This dog is Charlie.

Charlie likes to hide.
“One, two, three, come find me.”

Where is Charlie?
She must look.

"I will find you!
Here I come!"

Did he go into here?
Did he go out there?

She looks up. She looks down.
She looks under.

See that yellow?
That is a log not a dog!

Charlie hides too well.
Can you help?

Can you say, “Come out,
COME OUT”?

Out jumps Charlie.
"Here I am!"

What fun!

Good dog, Charlie!